Secret Kingdom

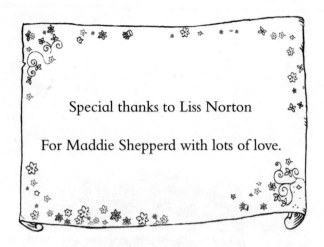

Special thanks to Liss Norton

For Maddie Shepperd with lots of love.

ORCHARD BOOKS

First published in Great Britain in 2014 by Orchard Books
This edition published in 2016 by The Watts Publishing Group

1 3 5 7 9 10 8 6 4 2

© 2014 Hothouse Fiction Limited
Illustrations © Orchard Books 2014

The moral rights of the author and illustrator have been asserted.

A CIP catalogue record for this book is available from the British Library.

ISBN 978 1 40835 301 1

Printed in Great Britain by Clays Ltd, St Ives plc

The paper and board used in this book are made from wood from responsible sources

Orchard Books
An imprint of Hachette Children's Group
Part of The Watts Publishing Group Limited
Carmelite House, 50 Victoria Embankment, London EC4Y 0DZ

An Hachette UK Company
www.hachette.co.uk
www.hachettechildrens.co.uk

Series created by Hothouse Fiction
www.hothousefiction.com

Ruby Riddle

ROSIE BANKS

ORCHARD

This is the Secret Kingdom

The Enchanted Palace

Contents

The Secret Spellbook

"Wow, it's amazing!" gasped Jasmine Smith as she looked at Honeyvale Castle.

It was a beautiful, sunny day and she and her best friends Ellie Macdonald and Summer Hammond were on a day trip with their families.

"I wish I'd brought my sketch book," said Ellie, tucking a strand of red curly hair behind her ear. "I'd love to draw one of those turrets."

"Let's head inside and see what else there is!" Summer said eagerly.

The three friends walked around the moat, which was sparkling in the sunshine, then ran across the drawbridge and under the portcullis that had once kept the castle safe from attackers.

"I bet this place was full of soldiers in the olden days!" exclaimed Jasmine

as they came out onto a grassy square inside the castle's high stone walls.

"Let's ask if we can explore on our own," suggested Ellie as their families came out of the gatehouse. She lowered her voice and added, "Then we can see if the Secret Spellbook can lead us to King Merry's missing ruby!"

The girls grinned at each other as they thought about the amazing secret that they all shared. They were the Very Important Friends of the Secret Kingdom, a wonderful land full of pixies, unicorns, elves and other magical creatures! They had visited the Secret Kingdom many times before to help the ruler, King Merry, stop his evil sister, Queen Malice, from causing trouble. But now she'd thrown the kindly king in prison and

snatched his throne, and the girls had
to find the four royal jewels from King
Merry's crown in order to defeat her.
So far, they'd found three of them – an
emerald, a sapphire and a diamond –
but the ruby was still missing and they
were desperate to get back to the Secret
Kingdom to look for it.

"I hope King Merry is OK," said
Summer anxiously.

The poor little king was locked in
a dungeon in Thunder Castle, Queen
Malice's gloomy home, and Summer
couldn't help worrying about him, even
though the girls had used the Secret
Spellbook to magic him a bed, an
armchair and yummy food to make his
cell as cosy as it could possibly be.

"Don't worry, we'll be able to set him

free soon," Jasmine said, giving Summer a quick hug.

"Shhh," warned Ellie, as her dad came towards them.

"We're going to look at the keep," he said. "It's where everyone used to shelter from attackers! Do you three want to come?"

"If it's OK, we'd quite like to look round on our own," replied Jasmine.

"All right," said Ellie's dad, smiling. "Just make sure you find

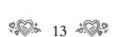

us before one o'clock, or you'll miss the picnic. And don't go out of the castle grounds."

"OK," the girls agreed. They watched as their families climbed the steps to the keep's door, then ran round behind the huge stone building to find a good place to look at the Secret Spellbook.

"Over here," said Jasmine, leading them towards an arched doorway. They ran inside and found themselves in a small room with narrow windows set into the thick stone walls.

"This is a great place to check the spellbook," said Summer, sitting down on the cobbled floor. "Nobody will see us here." She took the old, leather-bound book out of her backpack, and they gathered round it excitedly.

"I hope it has found the ruby," Jasmine said, crossing her fingers for luck.

Once they'd found the missing jewel, the four gems would magically create a new crown for King Merry. Then he would rule the kingdom once more!

Ellie quickly checked that nobody could see them, then flipped through the pages until she reached the finding spell. "It's complete!" she whispered.

Jasmine read the spell out loud:

"Something's lost that must be found,
Search through sea, air and ground...
To find the red jewel you must start
By looking in the kingdom's heart."

"The red jewel must be the ruby," said
Summer. "But what does *the kingdom's
heart* mean?"

"Wherever we're going, we'll have
to take the Magic Box with us," said
Jasmine. "We'll need the other jewels."

Ellie took the box out of her backpack
and looked at it sadly. Usually the
beautiful box was covered with pretty
carvings of mermaids and fairies, but
since Queen Malice took over, the
pictures had transformed into horrid
Storm Sprites and trolls. Worst of all,
Trixi, their pixie friend, couldn't use the

Magic Box to send them any messages, because as a royal pixie she had to obey the ruler of the Secret Kingdom, even when it was nasty Queen Malice.

"Maybe you should look after it, Jasmine," Ellie said. "If Queen Malice does manage to get close, you're the fastest runner out of the three of us!"

"I hope that doesn't happen," Jasmine said, but she took the box and pushed it into her own backpack.

The girls stood up. They looked anxiously at each other as they linked arms, ready for their magical journey to the Secret Kingdom.

"Let's hope Queen Malice isn't waiting for us," gulped Summer.

"We'll be ready for her if she is," Jasmine said determinedly.

Holding the Secret Spellbook open in front of them, the girls chanted the words of the spell together. The book began to shimmer with golden light, then lots of multi-coloured sparkles came whooshing out, lighting up the walls all around them.

The girls felt themselves being lifted up on a cloud of sparkles. "Secret Kingdom, here we come!" cried Ellie.

The girls gripped the spellbook tightly

and a moment later found themselves floating above the Secret Kingdom. Their special tiaras had appeared on their heads, although Jasmine noticed that they were still dusty and faded.

"There's Unicorn Valley!" cried Summer as they flew overhead. "And it still looks OK."

Not long ago, Unicorn Valley had been taken over by trolls and covered in horrible black mud and hundreds of stinky-sprout plants. Now that the girls had freed the unicorns, lush green grass and colourful flowers grew everywhere once more.

"And Sapphire Stream, look!" cried Ellie, as they reached the other side and spotted the blue water trickling between the flowery banks. "Queen Malice hasn't ruined it again. That's good!"

"And there are the Sparkle Slopes,"
Jasmine said, as they drifted over a
mountain range covered in glittery trees,
shining with diamonds.

"So the three places where we found
the other jewels are still safe," said
Summer. "But everywhere else…"
She looked down in dismay at the

empty, grey landscape below. Even though this was the girls' fourth visit since Queen Malice had taken over, it was still a shock to see the ruined kingdom.

"After today it will all be back to normal," Jasmine promised.

As she spoke they passed over the gloomiest part of the kingdom yet. The land was covered with thick black thunderclouds. "Is this the heart of the kingdom?" Summer gasped as they started to sink down towards the ground. "It's horrible!"

The Kingdom's Heart

The girls landed with a gentle bump. As the cloud thinned further, they suddenly realised where they were.

"We're in the grounds of King Merry's Enchanted Palace," gasped Jasmine. "But doesn't it look nasty?"

Queen Malice's magic had turned the beautiful palace's pink walls black and covered them with ugly gargoyles.

"I know they're made of stone," Ellie said with a shudder, "but they really seem to be staring at us."

"Can anyone see the ruby?" asked Jasmine.

The friends looked round, scanning the castle walls and windows, the bare trees and bushes, looking for a glint of red, but there was nothing but black and grey in every direction. Even King Merry's shining gold flags, which usually flew from the tops of the towers, had been replaced with Queen Malice's ugly black ones.

"Hide!" whispered Jasmine as a group of Storm Sprites flew past.

The girls crouched down next to the palace's black wall, their hearts thumping, but luckily the sprites flew past without spotting them.

"There are more up there," Summer said, pointing to one of the turrets. The Storm Sprites were flying around it, pushing and shoving each other and pulling rude faces.

"We'll have to try and stay out of sight while we search," said Jasmine. "We don't want Queen Malice to find out we're here."

She opened the Secret Spellbook at the finding spell. "Maybe this will tell us where to look," she said.

They read the spell three times, but no clue had appeared to help them find the missing ruby.

"Maybe we should look in the palace," suggested Summer nervously. "Perhaps King Merry's throne room is the heart of the kingdom?"

Just then, the huge entrance doors flew open with a bang and two trolls came lumbering out. They were massive, lumpy creatures with hunched backs, thick, stumpy legs and long, flabby arms that reached to their knees. Clumps of bristly, green hair stood up all over their massive heads.

The girls darted to hide behind a thorny bush as the trolls positioned themselves outside the palace entrance, swinging their long arms and looking around crossly.

"They must be on guard," whispered Jasmine. "Let's search the grounds before we try to get inside the palace. The ruby might be in the heart of the maze."

Keeping low, the girls crept towards it.

"Eurgh!" exclaimed Ellie as they passed the moat. She held her nose. "What a pong!"

Usually the moat was full of sparkling, sapphire-blue water, but now it was covered in grey pond-slime and hundreds of stink toads were swimming in it. As Ellie, Summer and Jasmine ran past, the toads gave them haughty looks – and one of them even stuck its tongue out!

The girls hurried on to the maze. The hedges had lost their leaves, but they were wreathed in black cloud, making it impossible to see through them.

"It looks spooky," said Summer anxiously.

Ellie squeezed her hand. "We'll be OK," she told Summer. "We've got the Secret Spellbook and the Magic Box to keep us safe."

"Here goes," said Jasmine, bravely leading the way inside. "Keep looking for any sign of the royal ruby."

"Wait!" cried Summer. "How will we find our way out? We can't save the kingdom if we get stuck in the maze!"

"Leaves!" Ellie exclaimed, picking up a handful of crumpled leaves from underneath a hedge. "If we drop a trail of these as we go along, we'll easily find the way back."

"Brilliant idea!" Jasmine and Summer smiled. They scooped up armfuls of leaves then tiptoed through the maze, dropping the leaves behind them as they went.

As they followed the twisting paths between the hedges, they peered all around, searching for a flash of red.

"I don't like being in here," said Ellie in a low voice. "I feel as though somebody's watching us."

"No one's watching," said Jasmine, but she glanced round nervously, just to make sure.

When they finally reached the centre of the maze, they found a large urn with curly handles standing on a low pillar.

"This must be the heart of the maze," Ellie said. "I hope the ruby's here."

They peeped into the urn but there was
nothing inside except a fat spider on its
web. Jasmine checked the pillar, running
her hands over it as she searched for
dips or cracks where the ruby might be
hidden. Summer and
Ellie peered into
the hedges on
every side.

"It's not
here," said
Summer, at last.
"Let's try the rose
garden. Perhaps
that's the heart of
the kingdom."

"The roses on the big bush right in
the middle of the garden are red," Ellie
remembered, "so they'd make a good

hiding place for a ruby."

They hurried back the way they'd come, following their trail of leaves, and were soon out in the open again.

The girls ran into the rose garden but were dismayed to find that all the colourful roses had been turned black by Queen Malice's magic.

"King Merry would hate to see this," said Jasmine angrily as they hurried to the bush in the centre.

They searched through the rose bush, turning over the grey leaves and peering at every flower, but there was no sign of the ruby anywhere.

"This is hopeless!" exclaimed Ellie. She sat down sadly beside the bush. "How are we going to find a tiny ruby in this huge garden? It could be anywhere."

"We need a clue to tell us where to look," Summer said, "otherwise we'll be searching for days." She sat beside Ellie and slipped her arm through her friend's.

"Maybe the Magic Box can help," Jasmine said, taking it out of her backpack. "Maybe the map will show us where the ruby is hidden."

The lid of the box flew open, revealing the tray that contained the six magical objects they had collected on their adventures in the Secret Kingdom. There was a tiny silver unicorn horn that let them talk to animals, an icy hourglass that could freeze time, a little bag of glittery wishing dust, a twinkling crystal to control the weather, a pearl to make them invisible and the magical map of the Secret Kingdom.

Summer reached for the map but before she could pick it up, the tray rose into the air, uncovering the three royal jewels they'd already found. They glittered brightly, lightening the gloom.

Jasmine reached for the teardop-shaped sapphire. As her fingers touched it, it began to shimmer and blue sparkles

danced around it. "Oh," she breathed, as a ball of blue twinkling light floated out of it, "it's so pretty!"

Ellie picked up the star-shaped diamond eagerly. Another ball of light appeared, silver this time and flecked with pink sparkles.

Summer gently lifted the crescent-shaped emerald and they all watched, entranced, as a globe of glittering, green light floated out of it and joined the other two. Then the balls of light began to grow and stretch, their rays twisting together, until they'd created a ribbon of beautiful, sparkling light.

"Wow!" cried Ellie, as the glittering light stretched up and up, throwing a line of twinkling brightness on to the castle wall. Suddenly they saw a glint of red

light at the very tip of one of the turrets.

"Up there!" gasped Summer. Her heart began to pound with excitement. "It must be the ruby!"

The Throne Room

The girls grinned excitedly at each other.

"The Enchanted Palace is the heart of the kingdom!" cried Ellie. "But how are we going to get to the ruby?"

"We'll have to get past the trolls *and* the Storm Sprites," Jasmine said, frowning thoughtfully.

"But there are so many of them," exclaimed Summer with a shudder.

"I think we're going to need help," replied Jasmine.

Summer and Ellie stared at her. "What do you mean?" Summer asked. "Whose help?"

"Trixi's," said Jasmine. "She *must* be in there somewhere with Queen Malice. We *have* to find her and set her free!"

"Good idea!" Ellie cried. "And I know how we can get inside the palace without being spotted." She tapped the Magic Box. "The pearl will make us invisible and then we can creep past the trolls and the Storm Sprites."

"Now we know where the ruby is, we should put the other jewels away so Queen Malice doesn't spot the light beam," said Summer. She pushed the emerald deep down inside her pocket.

Ellie and Jasmine did the
same with the other
jewels.

Ellie picked
up the
invisibility
pearl and
held it in
the palm of
her hand. It
shimmered with
mermaid magic.
The magic spread out
from the pearl until Ellie was surrounded
by a silvery glow then, suddenly, she
vanished.

"Where are you?" giggled Summer.

"I'm still here," Ellie replied.

Summer felt Ellie's hand slip into hers.

A warm tingle spread through her and she stared down at her feet, waiting for them to disappear. All at once, they vanished.

Summer reached for Jasmine's hand. "It's weird not being able to see yourself," she said.

"It sounds weird, too," Jasmine said, "hearing a voice coming from empty air!" Then she disappeared, too.

"We know the magic doesn't last for long," Summer said, "so we'd better head for the palace straight away. Let's look in all the windows to see if we can spot Trixi."

Jasmine placed the Magic Box in her backpack and they ran back over to the palace.

"We'd better tiptoe," Ellie whispered as

they approached the troll guards.

The girls slowed right down, then crept past, holding their breath. To their relief, the trolls didn't hear them. Jasmine, Ellie and Summer peered in the first window.

"It's the kitchen," whispered Summer. She was glad they were invisible because the room seemed to be full of Storm Sprites. They were flying to and fro, stuffing cakes into their mouths, or throwing them at each other and laughing nastily.

Below them, about twenty elf butlers

were kneeling on the floor, cleaning hundreds of pairs of the queen's pointy black shoes.

"Poor things," Ellie sighed. "It must

be horrible having to work for mean old Queen Malice."

"It won't be for much longer," Jasmine reminded her. "Not once we get hold of the ruby."

"I can't see Trixi anywhere," whispered

Summer. "Let's keep going."

The girls peeked into every window at the front of the palace, but there was no sign of their pixie friend.

"Let's go round the back," Jasmine suggested.

Holding hands so that they stayed invisible, the girls passed the lemonade fountain, but the sparkling lemonade had been turned to sloppy mud.

"Yuck," whispered Ellie. "Only Queen Malice could prefer mud to lemonade!"

"There's King Merry's throne room," Summer said. They tiptoed across a wide patio and peeked in through the French windows, which were slightly ajar.

They'd been in the throne room many times but now the enormous room was almost unrecognisable. The marble floor

was covered in oozing mud and slime,
and the ceiling, walls and curtains were
covered in portraits of Queen Malice,
staring fiercely into the room. All the
friendly elf butlers and brownies, who
usually waited on King Merry, were
gone. In their place were trolls, who
lolled against the walls, their long arms
swinging lazily, and Storm Sprites who
whizzed through the air, swooping down

to pull tufts of the trolls' green hair. The trolls yelled and swiped at them, but the Storm Sprites were too quick and zoomed away, laughing meanly.

Queen Malice, wearing a regal black dress and King Merry's crown, was standing by a large table covered with a map of the Secret Kingdom. A large troll, who towered above the queen, and a Storm Sprite wearing a soldier's cap

were looking at the map. The queen reached across it and tapped Fairytale Forest with her thunderbolt staff.

"Flubbart," she said to the troll, "take your troops to Fairytale Forest and dig up all the trees. Chase away everyone who lives there."

"He can't do that!" whispered Summer. Fairytale Forest was an amazing place where books grew on trees – Queen Malice couldn't ruin it!

Flubbart saluted. "Yes, Your Majesty," he said in a gruff voice. "And then can we plant stinky sprouts?"

The other trolls suddenly seemed to wake up. "Stinky sprouts!" they cheered, waving their arms eagerly. "We love stinky sprouts!"

"Silence!" the queen snapped. "You

can do what you like with the place
once the trees have gone."

She turned to the Storm Sprite in the
cap. "Drain the oceans, Blackwing,
starting with Dolphin Bay!"

"Oh, no!" gasped Ellie, horrified.
Dolphin Bay was the home of their
dolphin friends.

"We have to stop them!" cried Jasmine.

As Blackwing and Flubbart turned
to leave the room, Summer suddenly
spotted Trixi. The tiny pixie's leaf was
still attached to the
golden chain, which
was tied up near the
French windows.

Trixi was sitting
on it sadly,
holding her
little head
in her
hands and
looking very
miserable.

"There's Trixi," Jasmine whispered.

As the girls watched, a tiny tear trickled down the pixie's cheek. "Poor Trixi!" Summer gasped. "We have to rescue her!"

The Brownies' Hourglass

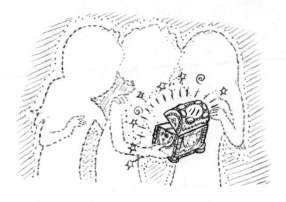

The girls moved back from the French windows. They were still invisible, but they didn't want to be overheard.

"How are we going to free Trixi?" asked Ellie in a low voice. "She's still a royal pixie, and that chain looks pretty strong."

"Maybe there's something in the Magic Box that can help us," Jasmine suggested. She took the blackened box out of her backpack and the lid opened magically, revealing the treasures hidden inside.

"What about the glitter dust?" said
Ellie. "We've still got one wish left.
Perhaps we can use that to free Trixi."

"I'm not sure," Summer said
thoughtfully. "Queen Malice's magic is
very strong. It would be such a shame if
we wasted our last wish!"

"I've got it!" whispered Ellie. "The
brownies' icy hourglass!"

Summer and Jasmine stared at her.

"It freezes time," Ellie continued. "So
that will give us a chance to talk to Trixi
while everyone's stuck. She'll help us
work out how to free her."

"Brilliant!" Jasmine and Summer
exclaimed.

Still holding hands to keep the
invisibility magic working, they ran back

to the French windows. Summer tapped gently on the glass and Trixi looked round dully.

"It's us," Ellie whispered through the door crack. "Ellie, Summer and Jasmine. We're invisible!"

Trixi's face lit up. "Thank goodness you're here," she whispered back.

Jasmine checked that Queen Malice wasn't looking in their direction, but the queen was still peering closely at her map. "Trixi, can you come over here so we can hold your hand?"

she called softly. "We're going to freeze time but we don't want you to be frozen too."

Trixi gave a tiny nod. She stood up slowly then steered her leaf towards the window, but the chain wasn't long enough for her to reach them!

The movement made Queen Malice look up. "What are you doing?" she demanded. "I didn't say you could move."

"I'm sorry, Your Majesty," said Trixi. "I thought I heard something, but I must have been mistaken."

The queen tutted, then turned to the map again. "Silly pixie. Anyway, I think I'll melt Magic Mountain next," she continued, with a cackle.

Jasmine cautiously opened the door a

little. She reached inside and touched Trixi's tiny hand. "I've got her," she said.

Summer flipped over the hourglass and dropped the pearl back into the Magic Box.

At once, the girls became visible again and everybody in the room — except for Trixi — stood like a statue. Queen Malice was frozen as she reached to tap Magic Mountain on her map and the Storm Sprites hung

motionless in mid-air.

The girls rushed inside. "We haven't got long," Summer said, putting the glittering hourglass down on the floor. "How can we rescue you, Trixi?"

Trixi thought for a moment. "I have to obey Queen Malice because I'm a royal pixie," she replied, looking sadly at the girls. "But maybe I shouldn't be a royal pixie anymore."

The girls gasped. Trixi had wanted to be a royal pixie ever since she was tiny. But they knew it wasn't the same without King Merry.

"What about the chain?" Jasmine asked practically.

"If you can find a freedom spell in the Secret Spellbook and I use my pixie ring at the same time, we should be able to break it." Trixi told them.

Ellie hurriedly flipped through the spellbook's pages, while Summer and Jasmine looked over her shoulders.

"The escaping spell didn't work on King Merry though," Summer said nervously.

"We've got to try," Ellie said.

Quickly the girls joined hands and read the spell out loud:

"Ancient magic, break this chain
And set this prisoner free again."

The Secret Spellbook began to shimmer with golden light and silver sparkles burst out of the page, whirling around Trixi.

"It's working!" the little pixie cried happily. She tapped her ring and chanted:

"A royal pixie I'll no longer be,
Pixie magic set me free!"

Pink sparkles whooshed out of the ring and mixed with the silver ones. As they touched the chain, the links began to snap.

"Hooray!" cheered Ellie. She jumped up into the air with excitement but as she landed, her foot caught the hourglass, toppling it over. "Oh no!" Ellie gasped. She tried to stand it up again, but the glass had cracked and sand was trickling out. Before the girls could move, the Storm Sprites and trolls unfroze.

Queen Malice glanced up sharply from her map. "Guards!" she screeched. "It's those human girls!" Then she pointed at Trixi. "You, pixie, put a spell on them! Quickly!"

The last link of the chain snapped and Trixi soared up to the ceiling on her leaf. "You can't boss me around anymore!" she cried. "I'm free, and I'm NOT putting a spell on my friends!"
She zoomed to the girls and kissed each of them quickly on the nose. "Thank you for rescuing me!" she cried, whizzing away again.

The girls exchanged excited looks as she raced around the room.

"Catch that pesky pixie!" shouted
Queen Malice at the top of her lungs.
The trolls and the Storm Sprites

charged towards her, but Trixi veered past them and flew on, laughing with delight.

"We have to get to the roof, Trixi!" Summer whispered to the little pixie, as she zoomed past the girls again. "The last jewel is up there!"

"This way!" Trixi cried. She flew towards the door and the girls pelted after her.

"Stop!" shrieked Queen Malice. She pointed her thunderbolt staff at them.

Hearts hammering, the girls ran faster than ever towards the large staircase, Jasmine leading the way.

Four trolls came lumbering towards them, but they were too slow and the girls dodged them easily. They shot out of the throne room after Trixi, just as a thunderbolt hit the door frame, sending sparks flying.

"Duck!" yelled Jasmine.

The sparks shot over their heads.

"That was close," Summer panted.

"This way," cried Trixi, zooming up a wide staircase.

A troll appeared in the doorway behind

them. As he turned towards them, his foot slipped on the slimy floor and he crashed down, blocking the door. The other trolls all ran into each other and

piled up behind him.

"That was lucky!" gasped Ellie, as she dashed up the stairs after her friends. She felt terrible for breaking the hourglass, but at least it looked as though they were going to reach the ruby before Queen Malice!

After running up three more flights of stairs, the girls finally reached the top of the palace. They headed out onto a high walkway, directly underneath the four palace towers. Each tower was topped with a tall spire.

"Where's the ruby?" panted Jasmine.

Narrowing their eyes, the girls peered up to the top of the spire nearest to them, but the ruby wasn't there.

"It's gone!" groaned Summer. Had Queen Malice somehow managed to get there before them?

Suddenly they spotted a red twinkle on top of the very furthest spire.

"We're on the wrong side of the roof!" Jasmine wailed.

"Don't worry," Trixi said, smiling.

"I'll magic you over there."

"Of course!" Jasmine grinned. She'd missed having Trixi and her pixie magic on their adventures!

Tapping her pixie ring, Trixi chanted:

"Pixie magic, use your power
To fly us to that distant tower."

Purple sparkles poured from Trixie's ring. Just as the ugly trolls came piling through the door, the girls quickly held hands and the magical sparkles lifted them off their feet and whisked them above the castle roof! Soon they were floating above the four spires.

Ellie gripped her friends' hands tightly and shut her eyes.

"It's OK, Ellie," said Summer, knowing

her friend didn't like heights. "We're almost there." She gasped as she spotted the heart-shaped ruby glowing below them, sending rays of brilliant, twinkling red light across the sky. But then she saw something else that made her blood run cold. A black cloud was racing towards the ruby.

"Ha ha!" cackled Queen Malice as she steered her thundercloud straight at the spire. "You'll never have the ruby. It's mine! And the Secret Kingdom will be mine forever!"

A Flash of Golden Light

The girls stared at Queen Malice in horror as she reached out for the heart-shaped ruby.

"Leave that alone!" Jasmine shouted bravely.

Trixi flew them down to the spire as quickly as she could, but it was too late.

The queen grasped the jewel – but her triumphant smile quickly changed to a puzzled frown. "It's stuck!" she complained. She tugged furiously at the ruby, but it was firmly fixed to the top of the turret.

Queen Malice peered closely at the glowing jewel. "What are these silly words inside it?" she snapped. She tapped the ruby sharply and sparkling red writing appeared in the sky.

Jasmine read it out:

"Think of something very dear,
The riddle's meaning will be clear.
The answer's sharing, caring, fun
For two or more, but never one."

Summer gasped as she thought about it. She looked at Jasmine and Ellie, who nodded. They knew the answer to the ruby riddle!

The queen scowled. "What nonsense is this? 'Something very dear? Caring, *fun*?'" She prodded one of her Storm Sprites. "Tell me what it means!"

The Storm Sprite shrugged. "I dunno."

The queen looked at the girls. "Do you know?" she demanded.

Before they could reply, her gaze fell on the Secret Spellbook, which was still tucked under Summer's arm. "The spellbook!" she cried. "Give that to me."

Then she spotted a corner of the Magic Box sticking out of Jasmine's backpack. "The other jewels!" she screeched. "Are they in that box? I'm the ruler of the kingdom and they belong to me!"

She swooped away from the ruby on her cloud and made a wild grab for the Secret Spellbook.

Trixi and the girls were still floating in
the air next to the spire. Summer dived
to her left, but she wasn't quite quick
enough. The queen caught hold of the
spellbook and tried to yank it away.

"Help!" Summer cried as she battled to
keep hold of it.

"It's mine!" snarled Queen Malice.

Before anyone could stop her, the queen pulled the precious old book out of Summer's hands.

As Trixi, Jasmine and Ellie floated over to help Summer, one of the sprites swooped down and snatched at the Magic Box, dragging it out of Jasmine's backpack.

Jasmine flew in circles, trying to get away, but it was no good.

"I've got it!" shrieked the sprite triumphantly, holding up the Magic Box. But as he cheered, the box slipped through his spindly fingers! It fell through the air, turning over and over. The lid snapped open and all the girls' magical treasures came cascading out.

"Catch them!" gasped Jasmine. She reached out to grab the unicorn horn, but it skimmed past her outstretched fingers, hitting the turret roof and shattering into a million pieces. The invisibility pearl landed in the gutter, then rolled down a drainpipe before the girls could reach it. The bag of glitter dust hit the roof, bounced off and shot away into the garden.

The weather crystal crashed down on to the flat roof surrounding the tower. A second later a panting troll emerged from a nearby staircase and crushed it under his huge, hairy foot. Summer stared in dismay. All their amazing gifts were being destroyed!

The map of the Secret Kingdom drifted down through the air more slowly.

Trixi quickly tapped her pixie ring and chanted:

"Magic map, please come to me
And shrink as small as small can be."

A fountain of rainbow-coloured
sparkles whooshed out of the ring. They
surrounded the map and carried it to
Trixi, shrinking it to the size of a grain of
rice. Trixi tucked it into her pocket.

"Ha! Serves you right!" Queen Malice
laughed as one by one the girls' gifts
were broken. "Now, where are the other
royal jewels?"

Jasmine felt a warm glow in her
pocket. *The sapphire!*

"Trixi, get us to the ruby!" she shouted.

The riddle was still written across the
sky as Trixi zoomed them closer.

"We know the answer to the riddle,"
Summer called to Queen Malice.

"You don't know because it's something you've never had!" Ellie added.

"The answer is FRIENDSHIP!" Summer, Jasmine and Ellie shouted together.

The ruby glowed more brightly than ever, then rose slowly into the air. Trixi caught it with both hands.

The girls took the other jewels out of their pockets and held them up in the air. As the four gems touched, there was a flash of blinding, golden light, brighter than anything the girls had ever seen before.

Air whooshed all around them. It smelled of strawberries, sunshine and freshly-mown grass.

As the light faded, the girls realised they were on the ground, with Trixi, in front of the palace. And in the air in front of them, in a bright patch of sunshine, hovered a new crown!

A Happy Reunion

The girls stared at the crown in delight.
It was made of gleaming gold and
the front was decorated with the four
royal jewels. They glimmered brightly,
spreading flashes of light across the black
ground. Wherever the light touched, a
flower and a few blades of fresh grass
sprang up.

"Wow!" gasped Jasmine, jumping up
and down in delight. "We've done it!"

Suddenly they heard a loud yawn behind them and spun round, startled. King Merry was lying on the ground nearby. He yawned again and stretched, slowly opened his eyes and then stared about him in surprise. "Where am I?" he asked sleepily.

"You're home, Your Majesty," said Ellie. "The Enchanted Palace."

The king leapt up. "Home!" he cheered and danced a little jig of happiness. He beamed at the girls. "I knew you'd rescue me."

Suddenly the crown floated towards King Merry and settled gently on his head. Rainbows of light shot out of it, making the girls blink.

When they looked at the king again, he was wearing his favourite purple robe

with white edging. His beard was clean
and fluffy and his cheeks had a lovely
rosy glow to them once again. He held
out his arms and the girls ran to hug
him. "Thank you for everything, my
dears," he said gratefully.

"We couldn't have done it without
Trixi," said Summer.

The king looked round eagerly.

"Has she escaped from my horrid sister?"

Trixi flew over, looking very sad. "The girls rescued me too," she said, hovering in front of the king on her leaf, "but I'm not a royal pixie anymore!" she burst into tears.

"Nonsense!" King Merry shook his head so fast that his glasses wobbled on his nose. "I, King Merry, rightful ruler of the Secret Kingdom, declare you a royal pixie again."

Trixi blushed with delight. "Oh, thank you!" Sparkles surrounded the little pixie as she stretched up on her tiptoes and kissed his rosy cheek.

"I've missed you, dear friend," said King Merry.

Suddenly Ellie noticed that Queen Malice was floating away on her thundercloud. "The queen's trying to sneak away!" she gasped.

King Merry's face darkened as he looked up at his sister. "Malice, come here at once!" he boomed.

"Never!" shrieked the queen, turning around and shaking her fist at King Merry.

Smiling, Trixi tapped her ring and said:

"Pixie magic, swirl around And bring Queen Malice to the ground."

Green sparkles zoomed out of the ring.
They settled on the thundercloud and it
began to float down towards the ground.

"Get off!" screeched the queen,
slapping at the sparkles. "Go away!
I don't want to go down!"

She landed right in front of King
Merry. The girls were delighted to see
that she wasn't wearing a crown!

"What are you grinning at?" she
demanded. Then she raised a hand to
her head. "My crown!" she shrieked.
"What have you done with my beautiful
crown?"

"King Merry is wearing it," said Trixi
happily, "and he's truly the ruler of the
Secret Kingdom once more."

Queen Malice stamped her foot
angrily. "That nincompoop!" she raged.

"He's a terrible ruler!"

King Merry glared at her. "Malice, give me the Secret Spellbook," he commanded.

"Shan't!" the queen snapped sulkily. "You can't make me and you can't force me to stay here either." She slapped at the magical sparkles that were pinning her thundercloud to the ground.

Trixi flew her leaf forwards. "Let me help, Your Majesty," she said, grinning. Tapping her ring, she chanted:

"No matter what the king might say,
Queen Malice must not disobey."

A fountain of multi-coloured sparkles whooshed out of the ring and whirled around the queen. When they cleared,

she thrust the Secret Spellbook into King
Merry's arms.

"Thank you, Trixi," said King Merry,
tucking the ancient book under his arm
and looking very cross. "I am furious
with you, Malice," he boomed.

Queen Malice snorted. "As if I care!"

"Look, over there!" said Summer. The
trolls were sneaking out of the palace,
dragging their clubs behind them.

The girls ran over to them. "Stop!"
they cried.

"Where are you going?" asked Jasmine,
hoping they weren't on their way to ruin
Magic Mountain!

"We're going back home to the Troll
Territories," said one of the trolls.

"We don't like it here anyway,"
growled another.

"There's too many silly magical creatures everywhere," said the first.

"And not enough stinky sprouts!" another complained. "We're hungry!"

"Good riddance!" King Merry said, shaking his fist at them. "Trixi, as soon as they're gone, destroy the bridge between the kingdom and the Troll Territories, so they can NEVER come back!"

"Yes, King Merry," Trixi said happily.

"And what about me?" asked Queen Malice sulkily. "I haven't—"

She broke off in mid-sentence as the king looked at her crossly. "This time I'm going to deal with you properly, Malice," he said in a stern voice. "ONCE AND FOR ALL!"

Queen Malice's Punishment

King Merry whispered in Trixi's tiny ear, then turned to his sister. "You have taken my crown, locked me in a dungeon, tried to destroy the Secret Kingdom *and* made the creatures of this land miserable," he shook his head sadly. "This deserves a very serious punishment. Sister, I have decided to take away your magic!"

The wicked queen's eyes opened wide

with horror. "You can't!" she screeched.

"I can. It's the only way to stop you
from being so terrible," said the king.
His new crown slipped over one eye.
He pushed it back and opened the
Secret Spellbook. The pages rustled and
fluttered to and fro. It sounded as though
they were whispering with excitement at
seeing King Merry again.

"Aha! Here it is, a spell for removing
magic." King Merry said, smoothing a
page flat.

"Brother, wait. I—" Queen Malice
started.

But King Merry read out the spell in a
loud clear voice:

"Ancient magic, take away
My sister's powers, now, today!"

The spellbook shimmered with golden light and Queen Malice backed away nervously. "Stop it!" she said shakily. "I know you don't mean it!"

The light grew brighter and golden sparkles whooshed out of the spellbook and surrounded the queen. She screeched loudly as her staff disappeared in a puff of white smoke, then her thundercloud vanished, too, dumping her on the

ground with a bump.

"My thundercloud!" she wailed, scrambling up. "Bring it back."

"No," said King Merry in a stern voice. "And there'll be no fancy yacht or coach for you either. From now on, Malice, you will have to walk everywhere. And you can help to clean up the mess you've made, too."

A broom and a mop magically appeared beside her. She tried to run away from them, but they followed close behind.

"Get these awful things away from me!" she commanded.

A Storm Sprite tried to catch hold of the broom but it jumped out of his hands and continued to follow the queen.

Queen Malice ran round in a circle,

but the broom and mop
followed more closely
than ever. "I WANT
MY MAGIC
BACK!" she
screamed,
stamping
her feet
in fury.
"AND I
WANT
IT
NOW!"
She ran her
fingers through
her hair,
making it frizz out wildly.

The king shook his head sadly. "You've
brought this on yourself, Malice."

Queen Malice narrowed her eyes. "Don't think you'll stop me by taking away my magic," she warned. "I'll find a way to pay you back, and then you'd better watch out!" She glared at the girls and Trixi. "ALL of you!"

She spun round suddenly, almost tripping over the broom, then stormed away, still shouting. "You'll be sorry! I'll make you pay!"

Her scowling Storm Sprites flapped after her.

The girls exchanged glances as they all disappeared into the bushes. Kind-hearted Summer almost felt sorry for the mean old queen, until she remembered all the horrible things she'd done.

"Let's hope Queen Malice learns her lesson this time," said Jasmine.

Ellie nodded. It would be lovely to be able to enjoy their time in the Secret Kingdom without having to worry what the nasty queen was up to!

King Merry closed the Secret Spellbook and turned back to the girls. "I don't expect Malice really will clean up the kingdom, even with the help of the magic mop and broom!" said the king. "Luckily, now that I am in charge again, the kingdom will start to heal itself and will soon be back to normal."

Trixi tapped her ring and the Magic Box floated down from the roof to land on the ground in front of the girls.

"Can you repair the Magic Box, King Merry?" asked Jasmine. She picked it up and stroked it sadly. It was no longer dull and tarnished, but one of the hinges was broken and the mirror was cracked.

The king gave a small smile. "It's still powerful," he said, "and, like the rest of the kingdom, it will soon mend."

"We've lost all our magical treasures, though," sighed Ellie.

"Not quite," said Trixi. She took the map out of her pocket and used her ring to make it grow again.

The girls looked at it eagerly.

"Look, the whole kingdom's recovering," Summer said excitedly. The black, gloomy lands were turning green again and they could see magical creatures dancing for joy everywhere.

Summer took the box from Jasmine and heard a rattle. Opening the tiny side drawer she saw a glittering purple gem nestling inside. "The Shining Jewel

is safe, too!" she said, holding it up to show the girls. The jewel was very magical and lit up any dark space with a beautiful glow. "So we still have *two* magical items to help us!"

Ellie felt a tingle in her hair. Taking off her tiara, she saw that it was twinkling brightly again. "And our tiaras are back to normal, too," she said happily.

A group of brownies appeared. They rushed over to King Merry, overjoyed to see him again. A herd of unicorns came galloping round the corner, their colourful coats and golden horns gleaming in the sunshine. The girls

spotted their friends Littlehorn and
Silvertail and waved happily to them.

The unicorns were followed by a crowd
of tiny pixies, flying full tilt on their
leaves, and elves hurrying as fast as their
legs would carry them. "Welcome back,
Your Majesty!" they all cried, laughing
and cheering with delight.

Summer tucked the map back into its
compartment in the Magic Box, then put
the box into her backpack to keep it safe.

Trixi flew above the crowd, smiling
at the happy scenes beneath her. Then,
with a wink at the girls, she tapped her
ring and chanted:

> "Let's have lots of fireworks here
> To show this crowd my big idea!"

Silver sparkles surged out of the ring and multi-coloured fireworks whooshed into the sky. They glittered brightly against the remaining dark clouds and spelt out the word PARTY!

Everyone stared at the sky, and King Merry clapped his hands. "I've just had the most marvellous idea!" he exclaimed, beaming at the crowd. "Let's have a party! We'll make it the biggest and best celebration the Secret Kingdom has ever seen!"

Party Time!

Ellie, Summer and Jasmine joined hands and swung each other round.

"There's nothing better than a Secret Kingdom party," Ellie cried in delight.

They ran to help carry tables out into the garden and were pleased to see the elf butlers pulling on their white gloves, ready to get to work.

Outside, they saw that Trixi's firework writing was still hanging in the sky. Suddenly the letters shone brighter, sending thousands of sparkles into the black clouds. The clouds drifted away, growing smaller and smaller as they went, leaving behind a bright blue sky and brilliant sunshine.

The unicorns lined up, facing the black walls of King Merry's palace. Silvertail stepped to the front of the line. "Ready, steady, go!" she called. Glittering magic streamed from the unicorns' horns and the palace turned pink, with King Merry's gold flags fluttering on top of the turrets once more.

"That looks so much better!" Ellie said. They dashed to help a brownie band build a makeshift stage from wooden planks and piles of bricks.

"Look at the pixies!" Jasmine said as she pushed a plank into place. They were zipping around the garden, tapping their rings and sending sparkles high into the air. Wherever they landed, trees and bushes burst into leaf, and flowers opened their colourful petals wide.

Suddenly a young pixie flew towards

them. "I think this is yours," he said
shyly, holding out a tiny bag.

"The glitter dust!" the girls cried.
"Thank you!"

"I found it in the garden," explained
the pixie as Summer put it safely into the
Magic Box.

Trixi flew over,
towing a large leaf.
Three brimming
glasses of
lemonade
were balanced
precariously
on it. "Guess
where these
are from," she
said, her eyes
twinkling.

"Not the lemonade fountain? Is it working again?" gasped Ellie.

Trixi nodded happily.

The girls exchanged excited grins, then sipped their drinks.

"Delicious!" cried Jasmine. "I think it's even tastier than before!"

They finished their sparkling lemonade before putting the last plank in place on the stage.

"Thanks for your help," said the brownies. They began to play a cheerful tune.

More and more guests arrived. Winged horses flew past, towing a huge banner with 'Welcome back, King Merry!' spelt out in glittering diamonds. More unicorns appeared, carrying delicious apple puffs topped with cinnamon cream.

The girls heard a loud buzzing sound
as a huge swarm of bubble bees zoomed
by, carrying an enormous honey cake
in a sling. Behind them came a column
of bearded gnomes, beaming cheerily at
everyone they passed.

Suddenly the girls heard splashing and a loud croaking sound.

"What's happening?" exclaimed Summer.

"It's coming from the moat," Jasmine cried.

They darted over just in time to see sleek creatures diving into the water.

"It's the otters from Sapphire Stream," cheered Ellie. "And they're chasing away Queen Malice's stink toads!"

Sure enough, the stink toads were leaping out of the water and hopping away as fast as they could.

"Go back to Thunder Castle where you belong!" yelled a passing pixie.

A trumpet sounded and an elf herald called out, "Let the party begin!"

What a celebration it was! It seemed

that every creature from across the Secret Kingdom had joined them, and they were full of happiness and joy to see King Merry again.

The brownie band played loudly and Jasmine began to dance. Soon a group of elves began copying her steps and everyone joined in!

King Merry wandered around chatting and hugging everyone. Trixi flew alongside him on her leaf. Every time the king passed a loaded table and chose something yummy, she put a pixie spell on it so that it would hover in the air beside him until he was ready to eat it. Soon he was being followed by a huge parade of cakes, pies and jellies!

At last the sun began to set over the Enchanted Palace.

"The party's almost over," Ellie said sadly. "Hasn't it been brilliant?"

"It's been AMAZING!" exclaimed Summer.

"The perfect way to celebrate the kingdom going back to normal," Jasmine said with a smile.

King Merry and Trixi came over.

"It's almost time for you to go home," said Trixi. "But first we wanted to say a big thank you."

"Indeed we do," agreed the little king. "Without you girls, the kingdom would have been ruined forever." He hugged each of them in turn. "Thank you from the bottom of my heart." He drew back and looked at them anxiously. "You will come and see us again, won't you?"

"Of course!" the girls exclaimed.

"Coming to the Secret Kingdom is the best thing *ever*!"

"If the Magic Box works now, anyway," Summer added, suddenly worried. She took it out of her backpack and examined it. The hinge was still broken, but the crack in the mirror was already starting to mend and she was very glad to see that the carvings of unicorns and fairies were back on the box, in their rightful places! She smiled, relieved that King Merry had been right about the box healing itself.

"It'll be back to normal before long," said King Merry. "And we'll definitely see you soon, my dears."

Summer put the box away and the girls joined hands. Trixi kissed the tips of their noses. "Goodbye and thank you," she said. She tapped her pixie ring and chanted a spell,

"Sadly our dear friends must go.
Take them quickly, don't be slow!"

Pink sparkles poured out of the ring and whirled around the girls.

"Goodbye," they called, waving to all their Secret Kingdom friends. For a moment, they could still hear the laughter, chatter and music of King Merry's welcome-home party, but in an instant they felt themselves being lifted into the air.

A moment later they landed with a gentle bump and as the sparkles cleared they found themselves back in the stone-walled room in Honeyvale Castle.

Summer looked round, close to tears. Ellie's and Jasmine's eyes were shining too.

"That was our toughest adventure yet," Summer said, hugging her friends.

"It was," Jasmine agreed, wiping

her eyes. "For a while I really thought
Queen Malice was going to win and
that the Secret Kingdom would be ruined
forever."

"But she didn't," said Ellie. "King
Merry is back where he belongs and
everything's OK."

The girls smiled at each other.

"Come on, let's explore before the
picnic begins!" Jasmine exclaimed. The
three girls linked arms and ran through
the castle. They were sure they'd be back
in the Secret Kingdom soon – and they
couldn't wait!

**Join Ellie, Summer and Jasmine
when they go back to the Secret
Kingdom for a**

Starlight Adventure

Read on for a sneak peek...

Ready for
Adventure!

Smoke drifted up from the fire. Jasmine
watched the flames dance and grinned.
The marshmallow on the end of her stick
was starting to melt and go crispy on the
outside. Even though she had just eaten
three hot dogs, her tummy rumbled. She
loved toasted marshmallows!

In fact, Jasmine thought happily, *this*

is the perfect evening – sitting in her pyjamas around a campfire with her two best friends, Summer and Ellie, and Summer's family. She snuggled deeper into the fluffy fleece she was wearing over her pyjamas. The autumn air felt slightly cold and damp and leaves lay on the ground, but she knew their cosy tent and sleeping bags would keep them toasty warm when they went to bed.

"I think the marshmallows are done," said Ellie, pulling hers away from the fire.

Jasmine nibbled a corner of oozy marshmallow. It was sweet and sticky and completely delicious. "Yum!" she said with a grin.

"Careful, Finn," Summer warned one of her little brothers who was sitting nearby. "Your marshmallow is going to melt completely!"

But it was too late. The marshmallow at the end of Finn's stick was already dripping gloopily on to the ground.

"It looks like a mutant marshmallow," said Connor, Summer's other little brother, inspecting it.

"It's the mutant marshmallow of doom!" said Finn in a spooky voice, waving it around on the stick. "Anyone it touches will turn into a marshmallow zombie." He gave an evil laugh.

"Attack!" said Connor. The two little boys started pretend-fighting with their marshmallowy sticks.

The girls squealed and hastily jumped out of the way as sticky marshmallow blobs flew around them.

"Finn! Connor!" called Mrs Hammond, looking over from where she was sitting with Summer's stepdad, Mike. "That's enough of that. Sit down."

The boys stopped fighting.

"Maybe it's time for some music," said Mike. He picked up his guitar and started to strum a cheerful tune.

"I love this song," said Jasmine happily. Part of her wanted to get up and dance, but she couldn't bring herself to leave her warm spot by the fire, so instead she just shut her eyes and began to imagine herself twirling in the firelight.

Ellie took a notebook out of her fleece's pocket and started to sketch a picture of them all sitting in front of their tent.

Summer looked into the trees and thought about all the nocturnal animals

who would be waking up about now –
badgers, hedgehogs, foxes. She wondered
if any of them would wander out of the
trees. She loved all animals – big and
small. It was so exciting to be there in
the woods, surrounded by them all.

Read

Starlight Adventure

to find out what
happens next!

Have you read all the books in Series Five?

Queen Malice has taken over the Secret Kingdom! Can Ellie, Summer and Jasmine find all the royal jewels and make King Merry rule again?

Secret Kingdom

Catch up on the very first
Secret Kingdom adventures in
this beautiful treasury!

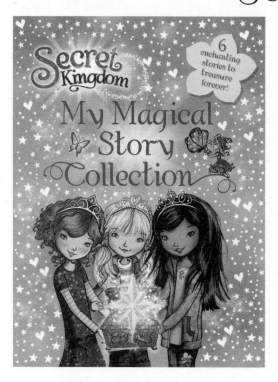

With gorgeous colour illustrations!

Available
September 2014

Secret Kingdom

Look out for the next sparkling special!

Secret Kingdom

Starlight Adventure

ROSIE BANKS

Join the girls on a special starry adventure!

Available

October 2014

Code Breaker

King Merry needs your help! Can you
break the code to help him remember
his favourite place?

__ __ __   __ __ __ __ __

Secret Kingdom

Competition!

Queen Malice's trolls might be big and mean, but they have a secret talent. All trolls love to sing...badly!

One of the trolls' musical notes is hidden somewhere in the pages of every Secret Kingdom book in series five.

Did you spot the note when you were reading this book?

Help Summer, Jasmine and Ellie stop the terrible noise!

Enter the competition by finding all four hidden notes and entering the page numbers at

www.secretkingdombooks.com

We will put all of the correct entries into a draw and select one winner to receive a special Secret Kingdom goodie bag featuring lots of sparkly gifts, including a glittery t-shirt!

Good luck!

Secret Kingdom

A magical world of friendship and fun!

Join the Secret Kingdom Club at

www.secretkingdombooks.com

and enjoy games, sneak peeks and lots more!

You'll find great activities, competitions, stories
and games, plus a special newsletter for
Secret Kingdom friends!